DATE DUE

MAY 03	MAY 25		
MAY 12	SEP 18		
MAY 17	SEP 13		
MAY 24	MAY 08		
SEP 30	MAY 16		
OCT 18			
MAR 08			
MAR 09			
MAR 16			
APR 18			
MAY 04			
MAY 11			
JAN			
JAN 16			
JAN 28			
FEB 22			
APR 06			

DEMCO 38-297

About the author

About the book

Insights,
Interviews
& More . . .

Read on

Meet Lidia Yuknavitch

About the author

Andrew Kovalev

LIDIA YUKNAVITCH is the author of the national bestselling novel *The Small Backs of Children* and the widely acclaimed memoir *The Chronology of Water*. Her writing has appeared in the *Atlantic*, the *Iowa Review*, *Mother Jones*, *Ms.*, the *Sun*, the *Rumpus*, *PANK*, *Zyzzyva*, *Fiction International*, and other publications. She teaches writing and literature in Portland, Oregon. Her new novel, *The Book of Joan*, will be published by Harper in 2017.

There Is No Map for Grief: On the Work of Art

Courtesy of The Millions

TRAUMA brought me to the page, it is that simple.

When my daughter died in the belly world of me, I became a writer—so that all the words that cannot name grief, all the words threatening to erupt from my belly and uterus did not explode up and through my skull and face and shatter the very world and sky.

Oceans of other people's compassions have washed over me, but those of us who have lost children, we are a living dead tribe. We smile and nod and thank people for their concerns and efforts. The labor of our lives is actually quite simple: stay alive. So that others might go on.

Wounds make artists. I wrote a book from the body of my dead girl.

There is no map for grief, but there are bridges to others.

When I was thirty and finishing a dissertation on war and narrative, a box arrived via UPS to the door of my home. The sender was my aunt—my father's sister—a woman I had become estranged from over the years for her ill treatment and unkind words toward me, my sister, and my mother. The box was about the size of a small television. I removed the brown paper and tape carefully . . . ▶

wondered why I had been careful? The cardboard box under the brown paper had a red lid. I wondered why. When I opened the red lid a hundred photos and yellowed papers and documents spread before me like hands. Nothing from my aunt—there was no explanation for what was inside the box.

Deep mistrust spread through me even as I put my hand down into the photos and pieces of paper. Something . . . a tiny electrical charge . . . moved up the crouch of my fingers and up my forearms and into my biceps and shoulders. I tilted my head to the side.

Then I took the photos out one at a time and looked at them.

I had never been to Lithuania, the land of my paternal lineage. But I am the only one on either side of my parents' families who has blonde hair. I have the square jaw and small blue eyes of a Baltic woman. I know because I looked at the photos, and they looked back. Myself. I saw selves who looked like me for the first time in my life. Even their bodies were of the shape and tune of mine—broad-shouldered and small-waisted, muscled arms and long necks and spines and Slavic noses.

I felt . . . secretly amongst people, when all my life I'd felt isolated.

But the photos were not alone.

Also inside the box were cut-out articles and Xeroxed copies of a story repeated over and over again.

The stories were about a photographer in Lithuania during the Russian occupation. This photographer managed to document a secret massacre at a hospital in a small rural town in Lithuania. With his small black box and second sight he had captured Russian soldiers shooting doctors point blank, the doctors' and nurses' dingy white scrubs speckled and blooming with blood caught in frames. Patients—some already on operating tables or in beds—shot in the heads and hearts, their mouths forever opened into "O" or "Why." Horrific imagery of mindless slaughter. Men. Women. Children. The uniforms and rifles of soldiers.

The photographer was my great uncle, I learned later.

He was then sent to a Siberian gulag for eighteen years for

taking the photos. But the Russian soldiers only found one camera, one roll; he'd secreted away the first camera and its secrets under a floorboard of the hospital, knowing his art was a death's head held carefully between his hands. From what I'm told, this is what "saved" his life. Otherwise he'd have been shot on site.

My great aunt hid the photos away behind the wall boards in her home in Lithuania at the head of her bed, in the long wait for her husband and his beautiful hands to return to her.

My grandmother hid the photos in her attic in Cleveland, Ohio, even as there were no more reasons to hide them I suppose . . .

My aunt found them when my grandmother died, and sent them, I found out later, because she knew I had an interest in—that my studies in graduate work were in—"war and art."

After receiving the photos I made a ritual. Every night I would walk to a writing shed to the side of our house. I would light a wood stove and bury my torso in a blanket waiting for the room to heat up. I would watch spiders that had spun new worlds in the corners or across the windows overnight. Occasionally I'd see a mouse going outside or coming in. I'd hear crickets and frogs and a creek's water making lines next to me. My husband and son safe and well in the house, the amber internal light of home making them glow from afar, the black and blue light of external night light taking me away from wife and mother and toward the body where I make art.

Every night I followed this pattern. This corporeal pull. A novel was coming from my body in images and rhythms I hadn't known were even alive in me—or perhaps they were coming from the dead histories living in us all. A novel that came from the box of photos.

For seven years.

I know a woman named Menas who is a painter in Lithuania. Though she travels to Vilnius monthly for food, to perhaps see an old friend, or for supplies, she lives in a rural area with very few people, a great many trees and streams, and regular visits from animals and the elements.

When I say Menas is a painter, you may wonder where she ▶

"shows" her work. What gallery. Have you seen her paintings? Is she on the Internet? Can we "friend" her on Facebook? But these are not the right questions.

When I ask Menas about painting, she laughs and says, "Painting is the labor of dream." There is nothing wrong with her English.

Menas lives alone on a falling-apart farm. In the past the farm was a Soviet Russia work farm. In the present the farm simply houses her as both she and the buildings do what women's bodies do . . . move away from children and family and scripted desires as the aches and pains and changes in bending and blood and bone toughen and wrinkle flesh, and hair—like wood—grays and weathers and thins.

Her paintings live in a barn that was used in the past for horses and cows and chickens and goats and machinery. They rest stacked against one another in great monuments to her dream labor, but haphazardly—nothing like an American painter's studio—more like history gone from the order of power to the chaos of ordinary wildflowers and moths and rodents. The paintings smell like hay and dirt and wood more than turpentine and linseed and oil pigments. Sometimes the dirt and refuse and perhaps even rodent or insect shit and probably even a spider or two gets into the paint before the canvas dries, and so her work wears an extra texture of . . . place. History.

The content of her work is difficult to describe. The colors, composition and imagery are abstract rather than representational, but that seems idiotic to say. I have now known her for twenty years, and so to speak to you in Art in America terms not only seems foolish, it seems worse. Like a terrible lie. Or injustice. To speak to you of her paintings I have to talk about bodies.

The body of her work is not an "oeuvre." It is not the end product or output of her artistic production.

Her body of work—her labor—is corporeal.

When I stand in front of one of her larger works, say, one that is 6' by 10', I feel "inside" a river, the river rocks rumbling under the soles of my feet, the ice of the water traveling up the bones in my shins to my ribs and shoulders and skull. Or I feel "moved" by wind in leaves, my body raising its hair and flesh toward the sky, and before I know it, I see that I've extended both of my arms out to the side of my body and closed my eyes and rocked my head back, as if to say, yes. Or I feel "turned" by the colors of fall leaves and that moment before the deep hues of gold and red and brown and purple decreate into winter's dead detritus. In these paintings I feel the land not "out there," but in my body.

There are other paintings. Larger than life and a little intimidating. It's hard to step up close to them, and yet it is impossible to stay away. I always end up touching them or leaning into them. Which one cannot do in any gallery that I know of. But in a barn, you can put your body against a painting. In the painting I am speaking of now I feel . . . like there is an inside-out. I feel a corporeal reversal. Like blood and flesh and the heart's beating and corpuscular surge have broken through the membrane we hold so dear called skin. The reds are more than red. The whites and blue whites and greys are nothing else but bone-colored—and they are cracked where they should be bold and hold. There are indications of vertebrae but they shatter the line of a spine. The blues are raging, bright lines that reach maplike and course and spread almost violently. Sometimes a more-black-than-black rage scratches from near the center and scrapes toward the viewer—looking almost as if it is trying to become a word, language.

There are no faces or bodies—and yet I feel more embodied than seems humanly possible when I am with these paintings.

When I ask her about the deep internal quality of these paintings, Menas laughs, and says, "It is not in words. It is body. Why words?" There is nothing wrong with her English.

When people ask me about Menas, I say I know a woman artist in Lithuania who fed her children on dirt and roots and potatoes and weeds and the milk from a cow and rain water for years.

Still they grew.

I say she loved her husband so much she carved his name on ▶

her own belly with a knife, and with the pulp and juice of wild raspberries, dyed it skin-true.

She had no money in the past. At different times she was owned as a laborer by the state. Her hands have touched many kinds of work. She has next to no money in the present, though she survives through excellent barter systems and trade with people who are still alive over time and history.

There is no story of this woman, of what happened to her, of how she came to be a painter, an artist.

There is no "news" that carries her name like a sensationalized trial on TV.

I can't point to something that will show you how important the work of her art is.

Is a painter a painter if no gallery or critic writes her name, carries her? Is a painter a painter if no one will ever know how art came alive in her hands, how painting day after day is a labor no one owns but her? Why should anyone care how grief birthed her art?

What is the work of art? Do we toil differently, me with my domestic and capitalistic trials and tribulations, and Menas with her chickens laying eggs, or the ones that try to lay eggs but hatch deformed things, the residual effects of Chernobyl something you can hold in the palm of your hand, her farm gone to seed, her family like a supernova flash that is an unrepresentable image?

We trade across time and lives.

Menas trades me paintings for stories.

She tells me in a letter, "Many thanks for your stories! They keep me! I am alive of them . . . " There is nothing wrong with her English.

Lithuanians, Latvians, and Estonians were primarily a rural people for centuries, their largest cities inhabited by other ethnic groups. The lyrics of their folksongs ring and rise with forests, mushrooms, animals, and azure-shimmering lakes.

Most Americans don't know how to picture the city dwellers in Vilnius—stuffed as they are with their big-boned and thick-muscled bodies in concrete apartment blocks as the heat turns their apartments into ovens in the summer and cold cells in the winter. We only know Vilnius from war stories and poets.

Most Americans can't see in their mind's eye the way the land pulls away from cities and urban dwelling and stretches out and away as if it could escape. Perhaps they realize the Baltic Sea licks the shores of the country, but isn't it freezing and inhospitable? Isn't Lithuania without mountains? Wasn't it dotted by Soviet farms and laborers? Most Americans have no idea what the new freedoms are for people who have been owned and traded and made into state property.

Menas tells me about saunas. A Lithuanian sauna is a mixture of Russian traditions and a kind of Finnish comfort. The bathhouses are usually two-story wooden houses with a sauna cabin on the first floor, rooms on the second, and a pond to jump in right after the sweat. Winter. Spring. Fall. Summer.

Menas tells me how to fill a day with fishing in lakes so cold and blue you can see the underworld of waterlife. How to ride horses across land knuckled with rounded hills and through birch and pine forests. How to spend long afternoons filling baskets with mushrooms or berries.

And in evenings, over email or in letters—the only letters I receive any more since in America no one pains themselves to commit to the old labor of letter writing—Menas tells me over and over again how her entire family was blown to bits—husband, son, daughter, in front of her eyes—while she held a basket of kindling for the fire, her hair blowing back away from her face and the skin around her eyes and mouth pinching with heat.

Each time she tells it, it is as if it is the first time. Each time (with a glass of pear wine or brandy at the end of a day, I know, because she has shared the smallness of the ritual, I can see the tiny glass going to her lips), when night falls and I am in the writing shed next to my beautiful family, my beautiful home, my appliances and computers and bills and cars and shoes and food and wine and cutlery that is "worth" more than her entire farm, she tells it to me. ▸

There Is No Map for Grief: On the Work of Art (*continued*)

There are plain ways to say it. When the Soviet Union fell, her rage and despair and grief took shelter in a falling-apart farmhouse. Alone in the labor of a life.

Menas says, "I become painter, to live."

But I think maybe it is simpler, her becoming. I think it is a choice to face not staying alive, with expression and labor and body. She is out there. Making new corporeal forms. With or without any of us.

Years ago, when Menas learned that my daughter died in the belly of me, she said, "Then you are down at bottom of water now. But see? You can walk the deep. That is why you here. Can you see me?"

Possibly the most perfect sentences anyone anywhere has ever said to me.

She is beautiful and terrible all at once.

I'm looking at a photo of one of her paintings right now. It is black and blue and as big as the wall of a house. Maybe it's the bottom of the water. Maybe Menas's lost family is there, floating or walking the depths, and maybe too my beautiful dead daughter. The image is arresting.

I must remember from her to push on the sentences until they break open and reveal all our otherness. I must remember to be a body that generates new ways of seeing and saying—the labor, the work of art.

A woman's body, without apology.

This language, held by the white of the page.

My daughter's name was Lily. ∿

An excerpt from
The Book of Joan

AND who did you think you were when they called your name?

Did you think you were who they said, the sound of your name lifting up off of your body in a great crescendo, the sound turning always to fever and ritual and chant, the sound of your name driving masses of men, women, and children, their teeth gnashing, their bodies falling forward toward their own brutal and quickening deaths? The mother kissing her son goodnight the night before the battle, the son still dreaming of talking animals, his sister's soft breathing through her small nose in the bed near him, the father locking the doors, as if everyone were part of a story that would make history, and not a story that would engender slaughter.

Did the white of your war banner give you the right to make murder a beautiful story? Who were you at sixteen, even your chest as yet unformed, your shoulders and biceps balling up like a boy's, your voice not low in your throat, but high, just under your jaw-line, a girl's voice, a cheekbone beneath the blue light flickering like some alien insect at the surface of your skin? When they mindlessly followed you into the fire of battle, when they shed their despair and aimed their hope straight at your face, when they turned their eyes to yours ▶

11

and surrendered, smiling, when you sent them into siege and seizure and bloodletting, in the moments before their deaths, did your valiancy outweigh your heart? Did you even have a heart? When you walked them into hell, was your heart open?

Did the song in your head give you the right to kill them?

Her vision blurred. Sometimes she saw things that were not there. She was used to it and not. Her head felt light and she couldn't feel her feet or hands. She looked up. When she looked back to her own reality she was in a floating room with slate-colored walls and floors. The windows black as space.

"JOAN?" Who would call out to her in such a room? But it was not a room. It was Leone, and the ground under her feet, and the smell of their rifles and of bodies that were recently made dead.

"Same firepower. From the past. Yes."

Joan watched Leone run her hand along the length of a single PG-29 rocket . . . she lingered on the small bone at Leone's wrist.

Ironic. An example of the very munitions she herself had used in Orléans. Years ago. A nine-day battle at the height of her command. Old dead wars leaving artifacts everywhere.

The CIEL bastards were using old earth firepower. She turned the tubular metal object over in her hands. She held the blue black metal cylinder upright. She smelled it. Dirt and death and alloy. She stroked the length of it. Its shaft a tandem warhead and rocket booster. She fingered the eight folding stabilizer fins at its tail. She spat on its metal side.

Fuckers.

The only place someone would need to punch through armor was down here. Not up there. Did that mean there were humans left? How many? Where? Individuals? Untethered civilian armies? Random feral children?

Wind skated the valley. In the distance foothills climbed up toward a low mountain range. In the past there was a rainforest rimming the rocky face of these mountains. But she couldn't remember the name of it.

Joan gazed once more at the dead men and pocketed the recorder and earbuds and looked up again at the night. Probably there was a Skyline near. There was always a Skyline near if there was a munitions station. The dark and thickened sky might obscure the view, but she knew what was up there. Invisible technological tethers dangling down to Earth like umbilical cords. The planet's population of Earth's elite above, now living an ascended existence away from a dying environment. CIEL.

Joan walked over to a field table under the canopy of the camouflage and rummaged around. The surface of the table was littered with plastic maps. Topographical maps. She spread her palm on one flat on the table and leaned over it. "What's this?"

Leone came close beside her and shone infrared light from the barrel of her rifle onto the map. "Looks like . . . what the fuck are those weird markings?" Leone laughed under her breath. "They look like fucking lightning bolts. Were these idiots just bored out of their minds and doodling?" Nothing but night answered.

Joan's mind fell backwards briefly. She looked out into the dark desert in front of them. Then over to the foothills and mountains. The climate of hemispheres didn't mean shit any longer. There were deserts and mountains and water. Sometimes. Maps were useless.

How many salvage missions had they traveled together in aircraft they'd located and lodged like vertebrae on a spine around the world? Collecting food and ammunitions and supplies for survival . . . at first with the assumption that they'd have to stockpile large quantities for their comrades, survivors, former rebels and civilians, maybe even enemies . . . but through all their travels and elaborate missions they faced a truer fiction: the people they found came to them in the form of a feral child now and then, or enemy combatants stationed few and far between guarding resource arsenals headed Skyward.

Where had all the people gone, they had thought. Was it possible entire armies, populations, had truly been atomized by geocatastrophic waves? Or were they forever subterranean, like Joan and Leone?

When the fuel began to deteriorate and run out it became absurd to continue to replenish it. It became absurd to maintain the aircraft and travel routes. ▸

Finally it became absurd to believe in roving bands of survivors. It was as if humans had devolved into processes of erosion, crumbling and sliding and disappearing back into soil and rock and dry riverbed. Or maybe back to their breathable blue past . . . into ocean and salt and molecules.

Joan shook her head and focused on the map in her hands.

Find and kill the Skyline.

Confiscate all munitions.

Blow what's left.

Get out.

If supplies were coming down this Skyline it was imperative to destroy it. If anything else was coming down, they were not prepared. Even with all the munitions around them they could not repel an attack at close range as a two-person unit.

Joan began collecting what she could of the ammunition. Leone followed her every move. As they worked the child's song wove through her skull. Moon, are you nothing more than a ball?

Right then an ear-splitting crack split the air around them. Joan clapped her hands over her ears and faster than animals dropped low to the ground. Leone crouched under the table and put her head between her knees. The sky lit up with red, green, blue light. More magnificently than any aurora. The ground rumbled beneath them.

Leone immediately positioned and fired into the surrounding terrain in short, controlled bursts. But her firepower disappeared into the night.

"Fuck," Joan yelled into the sound and light. Another cacophonous crack shattered the air around them. Even louder than the first. Her head pounded. Nausea. She felt something warm near her ear. Everywhere was a blast of sound and light.

Though she staggered like a drunk from the pain of the sound, Joan could see Leone quickly gathering up as many of the maps as she could and jamming them into her shirt and pack and pants.

"Let's not wait around to see whose coming to dinner," Leone yelled, already making for the boulders they hid behind when they came.

Joan gripped the PG-29 in her hand. A Skyline was ripping open. Right in front of them. If she didn't find it and hit it, they'd be dead. She positioned the warhead at the head of the RPGs. She squatted down on the ground and shoved the PG-29 down the shaft and secured it. Her brain was a bowling alley. There wasn't much time. She smelled her own blood. She hoisted the RPG up and positioned the shoulder brace. She gripped the trigger. She looked through the night sight scope. Blue and green crosshairs illuminated her vision. She aimed at the sky in the direction of the light and sound, but it was like aiming at a fucking aurora. She closed her eyes. Concentrate.

Find it. Find the sound.

The blue light at her head fluttered alive. A faint hum—a single low note—wove through her skull.

She turned to face the sky and opened her eyes to adjust the trajectory on the night sight scope once. Then she closed her eyes again and hummed a long steady note until it matched the tone in her skull, humming until she felt part of the matter of things, and then she dropped the gun gracefully to the ground.

Her shoulders shot back as if there had been recoil but she held her ground. When the force that shot out of her hit the empty night air, an invisible Skyline produced a dazzling fire-white line from earth to heaven, a jagged tear in the moment of things accompanied by a dizzying explosion. All the air around them and for as far as they could imagine detonated with sound. Bull's-eye.

Joan eyed the black bruise of night. Long wretched fingers of white and blue tracers streamed out from the blast line in all directions. An opera of chaos lit up the night. Joan could smell the fierce burning—the shorting-out of currents.

"Fuck you," she screamed at the sky and its drama. One less entrance and exit, shitheads.

As the light and sound show began to wane, Joan breathed heavy. She looked around at the munitions site. The dead men, the artillery and RPGs, the pack of corpse girls buried in the dirt. And Leone. ▶

An excerpt from *The Book of Joan* (*continued*)

Leone stepped close to Joan and reached up to wipe the blood from Joan's ear, then sucked her own fingers. "You taste alive," she said.

Joan smiled. Smoke dissipated. No light or sound surrounded them. Finally she could hear only Leone breathing. They needed to get back to the caves. They'd have to come back to retrieve the rest.

Leone picked up a second RPG and rocket to take with them. Joan turned to follow, her RPG back silently on her shoulder. Leone said nothing. They walked side by side. Dirt kicked up at their feet. Joan looked over at Leone's jaw. Somehow the square of it, the way she clenched her teeth, comforted her. ∽